Why Should k
All
The Fun Poems?

Written and illustrated
by
A.B.Wyze

2021

ISBN 9798505251058

https://www.facebook.com/ABWYZESTORIES/

CONTENTS

CATERPILLAR

The caterpillar crunched the leaf
and gave a little grin.
He thought about the warm cocoon
that he would soon be in.
He thought about the bugs who'd laughed
and called him Ugly Muggs!
For he'd soon be a butterfly
while they would still be bugs.

ORANGE DUNGAREES

I've got some orange dungarees
I wear them every day.
I wear them when I go to town
or when I'm forkin' hay.
I've had em now for several years
but they're still good as new.
And if you were to marry me
I'd get a pair for you.

I love my orange dungarees
they add a bit of style.
When folk around the town see me
they cannot help but smile.
But girl those beauties don't come cheap
they cost a bob or two.
But if you were to marry me
I'd buy a pair for you.

Oh man those orange dungarees
I sleep in them at night.
They hug the bits that need a hug
but never are they tight.
And if we get some rain at all
I shower in them too.
Girl if you were to marry me
I'd share that shower with you.

It wasn't very long ago
I took a holiday.
I sailed a boat right out to sea
and went and lost my way.
The temperature dropped thru the floor
but girl I did not freeze.
Thanks to the thermal lining
in my orange dungarees.

I've got some orange dungarees
I wear em all the time.
And if you do not marry me
well it would be a crime.
Cos we could have a family
oh say you will oh please.
Imagine all our children
in their orange dungarees.

CROCODILE SHOES

The ermine clad vixen
she stood at the counter
she tried but she just could not choose.
The green alligator
in trying to help her,
suggested some crocodile shoes.

"Oh, they are quite special,"
He smarmily told her,
"I'll even throw in a free hat.
They come from the land
of that Queen Cleopatra
you can't get more foxy than that."

He unpacked the footwear,
placed them on the counter
they looked so adorably sleek.
"They are quite expensive,"
his words flowed like treacle,
"but they are without doubt unique."

The ermine clad vixen
reached into her handbag
and brought out a fine snakeskin purse.
"I'll take them," she simpered,
"and if they don't flatter
I'll send round the boys with a hearse."

A rock steady rooster
who worked as a chauffeur
was smoking a Cuban cigar.
He put it out quickly
when he saw his mistress
and opened the door to her car.

The vixen ignored him
and stepped in the Daimler
then laid back her head for a snooze.
She dreamed of her neighbours,
she dreamed of their envy
once they saw her crocodile shoes.

The rock steady rooster
pulled into the driveway
the snow was beginning to fall.
The rear door was opened
his mistress was snoring,
she did not look graceful at all.

He coughed so politely,
she simply snored louder
and clutched at the shoes in their box.
The mansion door opened
the rooster turned quickly,
to see his employer the fox.

The fox wore a leopard skin
pair of pyjamas,
and bearskin bootees on his feet.
He walked past the Rooster
straight up to the Daimler
to look at his wife in her seat.

"I can't earn my money
as fast as she spends it
this Vixen is bleeding me dry."
He lifted the shoebox
then shook his good lady
who opened just one lazy eye.

"Where am I?"she whimpered,
"and what is the time dear?"
Her husband just curled up his lip.
"It's time that I shut you
away in your bedroom
this time you won't give me the slip."

The ermine clad vixen
she stared from her window
she'd never been so in the blues.
Her husband had taken her
store cards and burnt them…
he'd taken her crocodile shoes.

The fox was now dressed in
a fine sheepskin jacket
he puffed on a big fat cigar.
He opened the door
and he called to the rooster
to bring round the sleek Daimler car.

The green Alligator
was more than insistent
the shoes were now sold that was that.
The fox left the store
in a cloud of pure anger
and tripped up a cashmere clothed cat.

The shoebox was dropped
and the lid just fell off it,
the fox said, "I'm sorry my dear."
The cat gave a frown
and she looked in the shoebox
to say, "Oh what do we have here?"

"They're gorgeous," she purred
as her paw touched the footwear,
"they're simply divine and so sleek.
I've seen many shoes
in my time Mr fox sir,
but these are without doubt unique!"

The fox in the sheepskin
he knew about business
he recognised things such as luck.
He quickly invited
the cat for a coffee
to see if a deal could be struck.

The cat in the cashmere,
the fox in the sheepskin
they pulled up a couple of pews.
The fox was a sly one
he lied about prices...
the cat bought the crocodile shoes.

The rock steady rooster
drove back to the mansion
the fox spread the cash on the seat.
"I'll show that mad vixen
how businessmen barter
and then take her out for a treat."

They got to the mansion,
the rock steady rooster
he parked up the car at the door.
The fox in the sheepskin,
stepped out of the Daimler
and did not quite like what he saw.

He stared in amazement
up at his wife's window
a rope was hung down to the ground.
He entered the mansion
and called for the vixen,
but no one, it seemed, could be found.

He'd left in a hurry
he looked for his wallet
this wasn't at all what he'd planned...
The wallet was nowhere,
he did find a message,
composed in his wife's fairest hand.

"I've left you my dearest,"
the vixen had written,
"our future has come to an end.
For what good is money
inside a fine wallet
if there is no craving to spend."

And down at the station
where trains go to London
a wolf was admiring the views.
A catsuit clad vixen
with style and decorum
divine in her crocodile shoes.

ELVIS THE CAT

Our cat is now a vegan
he's put us in a fix.
For he will not touch meat at all,
prefers that Weetabix.

He eats that stuff for breakfast,
for lunch and dinner too.
Our cat is now a vegan,
and we don't know what to do.

We knew we had to have him.
We saw him advertised.
We knew that he was meant for us…
just something in his eyes.

The look he had was moody
that tied with our ideas.
We knew that cat would bring us joy
for many many years.

We called our moggie Elvis
it suited him so well.
We built that cat a mansion house,
The Heartbreak Cat Hotel.

We fed him up on burgers
on chilli hot dogs too.
We dressed him up in sequined suits
and pairs of blue suede shoes.

We gave him Elvis lessons
oh boy did he learn fast.
He curled his lip, he shook his hips,
he really was a blast.

His quiff looked really stylish,
he thrilled us both to bits.
We put him up on YouTube
and had half a million hits.

But now he's losing kilos,
he's thinner than a stick.
We know that we will have to find
an answer pretty quick.

Those suits he has now drown him,
he's too small for those shoes.
If we put him on YouTube now
we'd not get any views.

And then I thought of something
to save our cat's career.
Although he was so very thin,
the answer was quite clear.

Some sacrifice was needed
but that would be just fine.
For sacrifices must be made,
with stardom on the line.

We got rid of his mansion,
a minor thing to lose.
And then we burned his sequined suits
and all his blue suede shoes.

He still curls up his lip though,
and he still has his quiff.
And he still has his moody look...
We've changed his name to Cliff!

TO THE MOON BY BALLOON

I call my cat Montgolfier
as he can make balloons.
He inflates them with gentle purrs
and floats them to the moon.
And if you are his special friend
my cat may well decide,
to let you go along with him
and share a wondrous ride.

Beyond the brick-built bungalows
beyond the leafless trees.
Above the busy bustling streets,
transported on the breeze.
Far far above the traffic noise
where clouds obscure the view,
and out across the sandy shore
above the ocean blue.

I call my dog Escoffier
as he can cook a treat.
And he would take that ride with you
and bring something to eat.
You'll dine on pear and pecan pie
with oodles of fresh cream.
Then wash it down with raspberryade
that tastes just like a dream.

Montgolfier will sing to you
just like he sings to me.
The earth will soon be far below,
as tiny as can be.
And all the stars will harmonise
and join in with the tune.
Montgolfier, Escoffier and you,
off to the moon.

And when you reach the smiling moon
in all her silver grace,
Montgolfier will land you
at his very secret place.
There, in a cave of peppermint
and chocolate stalactites,
you'll sit and watch the earthrise,
such a truly wondrous sight.

Escoffier will rustle up
a minty chocolate treat,
and then you'll float back home again,
your day will be complete.
I call my cat Montgolfier
as he can make balloons.
And if you are a friend of his,
he'll take you to the moon.

WHEN I WAS YOU

When I was you
and you were me
and we were gelled...
Entwined.
When all things passing
did just that,
and left us both behind.
When time stood still
and memories
were something yet to be.
When we were us
and I was you
and you my love were me.
When yours was ours
and mine was yours
and you and I were US;
I lent to you my i pad;
now I'd like it back.......
no fuss

THE MARKET

The handbag stall is tucked away,
sheltered by the shrubbery.
It's as if they're shy of customers...
The owner is of Asian birth
skin like well tanned leather.
Facing up
or facing down
the winsome English weather.
Jumpers hang like paint charts,
dazzling to the eye
and on the breeze
the whiff of onions frying.
It's nine a.m.
and half the town
are shopping with their eyes...
stopping here and there
but no-one's buying.
It's like a side show being played
to engage the tourist trade
but they're still eating bacon
in their cosy B and B's,
waiting for the sun to come
and dissipate the shade.

The Market won't deny them this respite.
The Market, like a magnet
will draw those tourists in
and none of them will put up any fight.
And towels that flap like victory flags
will disappear in plastic bags.
Fish will fly from ice cold slabs
lobsters, shrimps and fine dressed crabs.
Sickly, sugared doughnut rings.
Hot Dogs for the cool young things.
Tender, tendrilled climbing plants,
ornamental Elephants.
Liquorice and jelly Snakes
jewellery...authentic fakes.
Matching scarves that look the biz...
his and hers and
his and his.
Bring the children, bring the wife
the Market will be succoured into life.

THE SONG OF ROBIN HOOD

Yes everyone around the world
has heard of Robin Hood.
A champion to poorer folk,
the man did so much good.

An outlaw in the eyes of those
within the palace walls,
but Robin fought for justice
and equality for all.

I delved into the history
of hero Robin Hood.
I pored through all the archives
to discover what I could.

My quest took me to Nottingham
where Robin fought his cause.
Opposing John the upstart King;
defying all his laws.

And then quite purely out of luck
I found a little chest.
And though it looked quite plain to me
it bore the Royal Crest.

It had no lock it had no key
but it was shut up tight.
I hid it in my duffle bag
and stole off through the night.

I took it to my cottage home
and showed it to my wife
who opened it in just a trice
with her Swiss Army Knife.

And deep inside the chest we saw
a parchment with a clasp.
I barely dared to touch it
lest it crumbled in my grasp.

We rolled the dusty parchment out
as gently as we could.
The faded ink revealed a verse...
The Song of Robin Hood..........

Robin Hood he did no good
he was not on the ball.
He took money from the rich
and gave the poor it all.
And then the poor were rich as rich
the rich were clearly not
so Robin stole it from the poor
and gave the rich the lot.

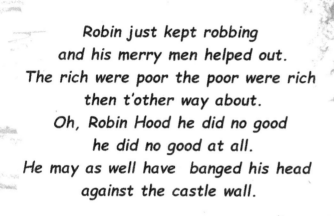

Robin just kept robbing
and his merry men helped out.
The rich were poor the poor were rich
then t'other way about.
Oh, Robin Hood he did no good
he did no good at all.
He may as well have banged his head
against the castle wall.

THE BORROWER

The final day of January
quickly rolled around.
My son came in to ask if he
could borrow fifty pounds.

February; shorter month
but ending just the same.
He appeared and asked
to borrow fifty pounds again.

March and April just the same
and just the same amount.
It became so regular
that I forgot to count.

On and on throughout the year,
I'd see that same young kid
holding out his skinny hand
and taking fifty quid.

My birthday in December
oh, he came around then too.
He said, "as it's your birthday Dad,
just twenty quid will do."

OH MY LITTLE AUBERGINE

Oh my little aubergine
I have some real bad news.
I have found another love
to fill your purple shoes.
Pray do not be miserable
we shared some happiness
I still regard you as a friend
or
just a little less.
But time moves on fair aubergine
and love she knows no bounds.
And I've discovered meat so rare
I'm eating like a hound.
I've said goodbye to salad leaves
I've ditched that nut loaf too.
And now I have regrettably
to say goodbye to YOU.

UNDER CANVAS

I don't know whose idea it was
I know it wasn't mine.
They said that it would be good fun
they said it would be fine.

I guess it was alright at first
and we had lots of laughs.
We played some games and played the fool
and took some photographs.

We cooked our tea on roaring flames
and drank a load of pop.
And up to then it WAS good fun
I wished it would not stop.

But now of course the night time's here
and we're all in our beds.
All zipped in this canvas tent
I'm wishing I was dead.

'cause there's no window in a tent
it's stuffy as can be.
And everyone is fast asleep...
and we had BEANS for tea.

DEAR GOD (The Message)

Dear God,
I have a message,
please help me if you can.
It's just a simple question
I've got here for me Nan.

Me Mum n Dad are rowing
they've torn the house apart.
They've dug holes in the garden,
and that is just the start.

Me Nan's flat's been stripped bare God,
me cousins have been round.
They've torn up all the floorboards.
They're searching underground.

I just can't take the pressure,
oh, God I've had my fill.
So can you ask my Nanny...
what she did with her will?

THE GREAT ESCAPO

My uncle was called Great Escapo.
In Europe he was a big star.
He'd wowed them from England to Turkey.
Yes he was the greatest by far.

And then he got called for the BIG one,
and he could not turn it away.
He climbed aboard HMS Mary
and steamed to the U S of A.

He went to the Empire State Building
to do the impossible stunt.
Escape from a case on the rooftop
then walk out the door at the front.

Magicians from east to west hailed him.
They called him the greatest of all.
He strode up towards the great building
as if he were thirteen feet tall.

He waved at the worlds TV cameras.
He drank in the cheers and the claps.
He knew that once all this was over
he'd be number one on the map.

"Escaping to me's second nature,"
he said with a glint in his eye.
"They've not made a box that can hold me,
I'll see you down here, by and by."

That man had more tricks than Houdini.
That man he was blessed with the gift...
And he would have blown them away man...
had he just not got stuck in the lift.

THE WANDERER RETURNS

I hardly knew me dad you know
he left when I was eight.
Me mum worked hard so we could have
some food upon the plate.

And then much later in our lives
a man walked through our door.
Me dad it was, it was me dad,
me dad it was I'm sure.

Me mum passed out, me dad walked in
to pat me on the head.
"I'm sorry I have been so late,"
me errant daddy said.

He asked me then how old I was
I said, "I'm fifty three."
He reached into his pocket
and he gave a gift to me.

Well I stubbed out me cigarette
and then put down me tea.
I started to un-wrap the gift...
whatever could it be?

But then me mum got off the floor
and staggered to her seat.
She looked at me she looked at dad
me heart it skipped a beat.

"Well you've a nerve," she said to dad
"how come you're still alive?
Most men come back within a year
but you took forty five."

Me dad he sniffed a pinch of snuff
and then he scratched his bum.
"I went to make me fortune dear,"
he whispered to me mum.

"I saw the state that we were in
and knew I had to act.
I did not mean to take this long
and that's a blooming fact.

But you have not re-married dear;
no boots behind the door.
So you are still me wife me dear,
of that I'm blooming sure."

"Oh I've had men," me mum replied
our vows are dead and done.
I've had three husbands since you left
and buried every one.

I've raised our boy from lad to man
he's educated too.
He loves his mum with all his heart
but he thinks nowt of you."

Me mum and dad both looked at me,
me dad began to stand
as I unwrapped the tiny gift
that I held in me hand.

Mum sunk her head in both her hands,
her elbows on her knees.
I opened up a tiny box;
I had two sets of keys.

"I've bought me son a house me dear,"
me dad said with a smile.
It's on the south Miami coast;
a beach house with some style.

I've bought me son a Porsche" he said,
it's just the car for him.
I've got the lad a girlfriend too
to pander to his whim."

Well mum stood up, her eyes were moist
she'd really got the blues.
I looked at her I looked at dad
and knew I had to choose.

Oh I love mum with all me heart
she's been me guiding star.
She never visits me and dad...
Miami's much too far!

A FRIENDLY CHAT

Just pop the old kettle on Mavis
I do like some cake and a cup.
I hear you've been down a bit lately
I thought I might just cheer you up.

I've not been too brilliant Mavis,
had aches where they shouldn't have been.
If you ever get to my age gal
well then you'll know just what I mean.

I made an appointment with doctor.
You can't pick the one you will see.
I bet I get lumbered with new one,
he can't be above twenty-three.

My Ted's up there twice a week Mavis,
he sits there with all the old dears.
They talk but he don't hear a word gal
for all of that wax in his ears.

And tablets, don't talk about tablets
oh Mavis he's boxes o' those.
And ointments for dark hidden places
and sprays for his ears and his nose.

I said gal he's twice a week up there,
I hardly get up there meself.
If doctor gives me a prescription
I couldn't find room on the shelf!

Oh I clap me hands to them doctors
and all them cures what they have found.
Oh Mave if it weren't for them experts
my Ted'd be well underground.

Oh no gal he'll not be cremated
he never could bear it too hot.
We've had words with parson at church Mave
we've paid for our own private plot.

Oh aye I'll be buried beside him,
we'll both have a smart marble stone.
And service is all tekk'n care of.
It's paid for it isn't a loan.

No we don't go in for cremation
it might be alright for some folk.
I don't rate their chances in Heaven
if wind catches hold o' their smoke.

And though you're much younger than me Mave
that reaper does just as he likes.
You ought to start making arrangements,
we none of us know when he'll strike.

Take young Brenda Boothroyd for instance
she weren't a day older than you.
She went down to sign for Weight Watchers
and then popped her clogs in the queue.

But she weren't cremated our Mavis.
In her case it should have been done.
That Brenda were size of a whale gal
her box must've weighed half a ton!

Well thanks for the chat I'll be off now
I'm due up the doctors at four.
I DO hope that I cheered you up gal
well Mave, ain't that what friends are for?

CHICKENS

Chickens don't fly
even though they have wings
to them
just the thought of it sickens.
No,
chickens are more scared of flying than I
I s'pose it is why
they're called chickens.

MOUNTAINS OF SAND

Now the rock on the shore's
not a rock any more
for the ocean got angry with it.
And it washed at the rock,
every hour round the clock,
and the rock wore away bit by bit.

For a year and a day
the sea battered away,
and the rock could do nothing but stand.
Now the rock on the shore's
not a rock anymore
it's been changed into small grains of sand.

Now the sand on the shore
isn't there any more,
for the men came and gathered it all.
And they mixed it around
with cement on the ground
and they used it to build a huge wall.

And they built up the wall
till it stood strong and tall,
and they smiled for the sea had been tricked.
But the sea twice a day
simply pounded away,
at the wall made from mortar and brick.

Now the wall on the shore's
not a wall any more,
and the men have moved further inland.
But their children adore
coming down to the shore
and they play in the mountains of sand.

DOCTOR FIX IT

I wrote down my problems,
it took me some time.
It read like an
A to Z booklet on crime.

I went to my doctor
I showed him my list.
He joked, "are you sure
there is nothing you've missed?

You're perfectly healthy
and you don't need me,
it's all superficial
you have to agree."

I said, "You're my doctor
and I must protest.
You must do your duty
and run up some tests."

My doctor he tutted
and then he just sighed.
"You're perfectly healthy,
it can't be denied."

But when I insisted
that I was a wreck,
he promised to give me
a once over check.

"Your face is not perfect
but no-one has that.
Your ears would hear well
if you took off your hat.

Your teeth could just do
with a mild dental floss,
those spots on your hands
are Magnolia Gloss.

Your pulse is quite normal,
your watch runs too fast.
Your legs would be warm
if your pants weren't half mast.

Don't wear such tight shoes
and you might feel your toes.
Your sneezing is down
to those hairs up your nose.

You're not overweight
but your wallet is fat."
He gave me my bill
and he cured me of THAT!

THE CURIOUS CHILD

The crocodile smiled
at the curious child
who clung to
the bars of the cage.

The crocodile grinned
as he tried to climb in,
so plump
for a boy of his age.

The crocodile smirked
at the
stupid young jerk
who wanted to...
"Count cwoccies teggies."

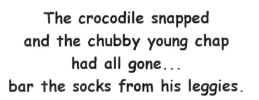

The crocodile snapped
and the chubby young chap
had all gone...
bar the socks from his leggies.

AN ALLIGATOR ATE A GOAT

An alligator ate a goat
an alligator did,
he slipped that goat
straight down his throat
then ran away and hid.
And this upset the marmoset
who told the old gnu,
who told the fox upon his box
who blew his didgeridoo.
And this disturbed the zebra herd
who ran into the trees,
they told a frog who told a hog
who told the chimpanzees.
The chimpanzees were not too pleased
they had to pass it on.
They told a jay who straight away
sang such a sad, sad song.
And this distressed the lioness
who burst out into tears.
And then of course the river horse
just covered up his ears.

And this no doubt intrigued the trout
who told the honey bee,
who told the drake, who told the snake
that lived inside a tree
The snake it sneaked down to the creek
to tell the alligator.
Oh, poor old snake, a BIG mistake...
The alligator ate her.
The alligator ate a snake
its tail up to its head.
Snake and skin with poison in...
The alligator's dead!

STORIES (Part One)

This is the story of Barnabus Bright
who turned to the left
when he should have turned right.
Who walked up the hill
when he should have walked down.
Who came to the meadow
just outside of town.

Who foolishly spoke
when he should have been quiet.
Who asked of the wolf
what he ate in his diet.
Who has not been seen
since that dark fateful night...
So ends the story
of Barnabus Bright.

This is the story of Caroline Kerr
who said there was nobody
better than her.
Who knew people suffered
but just did not care.
Who walked with her nose
stuck high in the air.

Who said she could do something
really absurd.
Who walked off the clifftop
to fly like a bird.
And that was the last
we all saw of her.
So ends the story
of Caroline Kerr.

This is the story of Pamela Pease
who never said thank you
and never said please.
Who went to the wood
with one thing on her mind,
to pester the very first
thing she could find.

Who picked on a worm,
what an awful mistake.
That worm was no worm
but a twenty foot snake.
She did not feel pleased
when it gave her a squeeze...
So ends the story
of Pamela Pease.

This is the story of Vera De Veere
who walked over there
when she should have come here.
Who then travelled east
when she should have gone west.
Who always insisted
she knew what was best.

Who went to the bridge
and tossed twigs in the brook.
Who should have run off
but decided to look.
Who spoke to the troll
with the long pointed spear...
So ends the story
of Vera De Veere.

THE PLAN

THE PLAN

I had a plan
a wicked plan
I did not tell a soul.
I took the tube
I took a bus
to get me to my goal.
I had the fangs
I had the blood
I'd practised with my scream.
The coast looked clear
I climbed the wall
my plan went like a dream.
I reached the door
and I knocked hard
but then my plan went wrong.
A man who looked
just like James Bond
he slipped the handcuffs on.
They dragged me off
and locked me up
I missed all Halloween.
And all because
I had a plan
to trick or treat the Queen.

THE CONTINUING STORY OF HUMPTY DUMPTY

Oh dear, Humpty Dumpty
all over he lay
with bits in the duck pond
and bits in the hay.

And bits by the roadside
and bits by the wall.
It couldn't have been
a more terrible fall.

The people of Toy Town
just stood by and stared.
Not one of them knew
how to get him repaired.

And then, Simple Simon,
he came into view,
he carried a paste brush
and bucket of glue.

He picked up the pieces
and stuck them with glue.
He put Humpty back, saying,
"You're good as new."

The people of Toy Town
they stared at the egg.
His legs were now arms
and his arms were now legs.

Then two naughty children
who everyone knew
yes, Little Jack Horner
and Little Boy Blue.

They climbed up to play
with the jumbled up egg.
They pinched on his arms
and they punched at his legs.

The North Wind looked on
and she scowled at these two
she started to blow,
and she blew and she blew!

She blew them both up
and she blew them both down.
They broke into two
as they hit the hard ground.

The people of Toy Town
just hadn't a clue
no-one had any
idea what to do.

And all the Kings horses
and all the King's men,
could not put the boys
back together again.

And then Simple Simon
came back into view,
he still had his paste brush;
he still had some glue.

He stuck the boys up
and he made them anew...
Yes...Little BOY Horner
and Little Jack BLUE!

DECISIONS

Have you ever turned left
when you should have turned right?
Or slept through the daytime
and not through the night?
Have you ever stood up
when you should have stood back?
Have you ever played red
when you should have played black?
Have you ever said yes
when you should have said no?
Have you ever pitched high
when you should have pitched low?
Have you ever stayed in
when you should have gone out?
Have you ever been sure
when you should have had doubt?
Have you ever moved fast
when you should have moved slow?
Have you ever called STOP
when you should have said go?
Have you ever been mad
when you should have been calm?
Have you ever raised hope
when it should be alarm?
Have you ever stood still
when you should just take flight?
Have you ever turned left
when you should have turned right?

SHOOT

L.H.O. shot J.F.K
in Dallas, in that car.
J.R. then shot L.H.O.
but no one shot J.R.

THE TERRIBLE FATE OF CHARLIE BONE

Charlie Bone weighed
just four stones
he strolled
onto the green.
Some had been
and some had gone
but none
had looked this keen.

The wind was like a hurricane
it rushed in from the sea.
Poor Charlie Bone could hardly stand,
he hung on to a tree.

But there are certain rules you see
if you should fly a kite
and Charlie did not realise
his weight was far too slight.

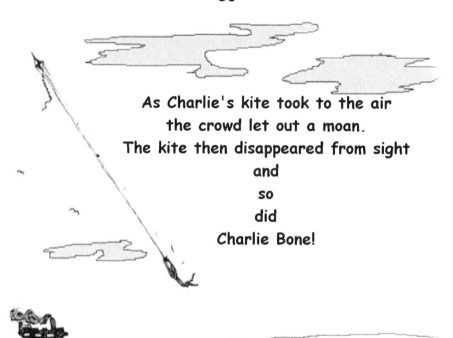

As Charlie's kite took to the air
the crowd let out a moan.
The kite then disappeared from sight
and
so
did
Charlie Bone!

The lifeguard was alerted
and the R.A.F. were phoned.
The Royal Navy searched the sea
for poor old Charlie Bone.

Charlie Bone weighed
just four stones
his kite did come to rest.
High upon Ben Nevis
in a golden eagle's nest.

The eagle had
two hungry chicks
which sealed poor Charlie's fate.
Soon Charlie Bone weighed nothing
but
those chicks
did put on weight.

SUMMER WORKOUT

We have to start our training
we do it once a year.
A rigid fitness programme
to get us into gear.

So, goodbye tapioca
and goodbye fish and chips.
We'll see you in the autumn,
you must not pass our lips.

We've dusted off the bikes now
we know it will be hard.
We cycle every morning
along the promenade.

We're both of us past sixty
we've gained a pound or three.
The good life in Hunstanton,
relaxing by the sea.

So goodbye chocolate sundae,
goodbye to all ice cream.
We have to start our training.
Our get fit quick regime.

Those yoghurts are on offer
it's buy one get one free.
We eat them every day now
with sticks of celery.

My wife is pumping iron...
she does not plug it in.
We have to get much fitter,
we used to be so thin.

So, goodbye all beefburgers,
auf wiedersehen real ale.
Our plates are piled with spinach
and crispy curly kale.

We don't drive to the shops now
we're jogging there instead
and if the milk gets curdled
we use it as a spread.

And yes, there is a reason
for this activity.
A rigid health food diet
increases energy.

We're toning up our bodies
to reach our fitness peak.
Our grandkids will be here soon
we've got them for two weeks!

FROG'S LEGS FOR TEA

They don't cook their fish in Japan.
They eat it as fresh as they can.
They catch it, and clean it,
and give it a slice;
then serve it with seaweed,
all rolled up with rice.
And I say that it's a brave man;
who'll go and eat fish in Japan.
In France it's a different tale.
For there they eat frog's legs and snails.
They cook them in
so many regional ways,
then serve them with garlic,
that lingers for days.
From Paris right down to Marseilles;
they're eating
those frog's legs and snails.
In England the frogs all jump free;
and snails are as safe as can be.
And fish; Oh I'm drooling,
I'm licking my lips,
it's deep fried in batter,
and served up with chips.
I'm sure that you all must agree;
that's better than frog's legs for tea.

LOST IN SPACE

High above the fields of snow
and high above the trees.
Leaving buildings far below
they're flying with such ease.

Far above the planet Earth,
on through the winter night.
Faster, faster, faster still,
they're almost out of sight.

Hear the reindeer panting hard,
and hear the sleigh bells ring.
Hear the voice of Santa shout...
"How do you STOP this blooming thing?"

STORIES (Part Two)

This is the story of Harriet Hook
who never did anything
quite by the book.
Who cheated her way
to the top of the heap.
Who robbed her own granny
while she was asleep.

Who never did anything
she had been told.
Who rowed up the Amazon
searching for gold.
One fast alligator
was all that it took.
So ends the story of Harriet Hook.

This is the story of Benjamin Bunn
who went for a walk...
(too fat to run.)
Who walked really slowly
but should have walked fast.
Who entered the cave
but should have walked past.

Who squeezed his plump body
to get through the gap.
Who woke the old grizzly bear
up from his nap.
That bear was so grateful
for what Ben had done.
So ends the story of Benjamin Bunn.

This is the story of Claudia Clott
who said that it was
when she knew it was not.
Who said it was black
even though it was white.
Who went for a walk
on the stroke of midnight.

Who laughed at the witch
on her willowy broom.
Who followed her back
to her dark smoky room.
That witch had a cauldron
all steaming and hot.
So ends the story of Claudia Clott.

This is the story of Wilberforce Weed
who always took more
than he'd ever need.
Who then took a mile
when they gave him a yard.
Who dropped all his friends
on the turn of a card.

Who went to the ocean
to take a long swim.
And that was the last
that we all saw of him.
Those sharks were quite hungry
and fancied a feed.
So ends the story of Wilberforce Weed.

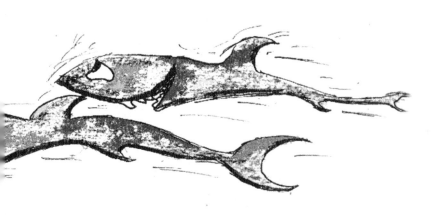

EMBELLISHMENT

Tom he told Tyne
who then told it to Tim,
who telephoned Henry,
and told it to him.
Henry told Herbert
and Herbert told Hugh
who told it to Davy,
what else could he do?
Davy told Dora
and Dora told Dom
who ran like a demon,
to tell it to Tom.
The story had altered
so much in this time
that Tom hurried over
to tell it to Tyne.

KIDS, EH?

"We've got a question Dad."
enquired the little boys.
"When Santa was a lad
who brought him all his toys?"

THE END

Printed in Great Britain
by Amazon

62106101R00047